MW00883189

Gene Kemp's first books for children, a series of stories about an amazing pig called Tamworth, immediately established her as one of the funniest and most imaginative authors writing for young people. Then she wrote *The Turbulent Term of Tyke Tiler*, a ground-breaking school story which won the Library Association's Carnegie Medal and the Other Award and shot to the top of the children's bestseller lists. Other titles set in Cricklepit Combined School followed. Collections of short stories, novels for teenagers, fiction for younger children and a powerful narrative poem, *The Mink War*, have all added to her reputation as one of the most popular contemporary children's authors. In recognition of her achievement as a writer of children's books she was awarded an honorary degree in 1984. She lives in Exeter in Devon.

by the same author

Poetry for Children

DUCKS AND DRAGONS
THE MINK WAR

Fiction for Children

THE TURBULENT TERM OF TYKE TILER
(Awarded the Library Association's Carnegie Medal)

GOWIE CORBY PLAYS CHICKEN
CHARLIE LEWIS PLAYS FOR TIME
(Runner-up for the Whitbread Award)

JUNIPER: A MYSTERY
JUST FERRET
JASON BODGER AND THE PRIORY GHOST
MR MAGUS IS WAITING FOR YOU
DOG DAYS AND CAT NAPS
THE CLOCK TOWER GHOST
THE WELL
THE PRIME OF TAMWORTH PIG
TAMWORTH PIG SAVES THE TREES
TAMWORTH PIG AND THE LITTER
CHRISTMAS WITH TAMWORTH PIG
NO PLACE LIKE
I CAN'T STAND LOSING
THE ROOM WITH NO WINDOWS
ROUNDABOUT

Tamworth Pig Rides Again!
GENE KEMP

Illustrated by Carolyn Dinan

faber and faber
LONDON · BOSTON

First published in 1992
by Faber and Faber Limited
3 Queen Square London WC1N 3AU
This paperback edition first published in 1994

Printed in England by Clays Ltd, St Ives plc

All rights reserved

© Gene Kemp, 1992
Illustrations © Carolyn Dinan, 1992

Gene Kemp is hereby identified as author of this work
in accordance with Section 77 of the Copyright, Designs
and Patents Act 1988

*This book is sold subject to the condition that it shall not, by way of trade
or otherwise, be lent, resold, hired out or otherwise circulated without the
publisher's prior consent in any form of binding or cover other than that
in which it is published and without a similar condition including
this condition being imposed on the subsequent purchaser.*

A CIP record for this book is available from the British Library.

ISBN 0 571 17218 0

2 4 6 8 10 9 7 5 3 1

For Gerald Pollinger,
with love

Ah! Tamworth Pig is a very fine pig
  The best you'll ever see,
His ears stand up, his snout is long,
  His score is twenty-three.
He's wise and good and big and bold,
  And clever as can be,
A faithful friend to young and old
  The Pig of Pigs is he.

By courtesy of Mr Rab

Chapter One

Thomas dribbled a tennis ball very neatly down the road, whistling 'Nice one, Cyril' as he did so. The ball belonged to his sister, Blossom, but he had temporarily borrowed it, because he had lost his own football and he wanted to have a game with his friend Henry. Blossom didn't like him to borrow her ball, but then she didn't know, so it wouldn't matter. His whistle moved to a higher, more piercing note as he brilliantly stopped the ball from flying off the pavement. Thomas felt full of cheer. Soon it would be the end of term, and then . . . the holidays! Fantastic, fabulous holidays. Dozens of school-free days. The idea filled him with such splendiferous bliss that his foot swung high, kicking the ball with tremendous power.

It sailed straight over the wall into the nearest garden, and Thomas's spirits fell to zero – splat. He stopped whistling, all happiness gone. For the garden into which Blossom's ball had flown belonged to Mrs Twitchie, the Headmistress of Thomas's school. Now, in Thomas's life there were many hates, but Mrs Twitchie came high, very high, on the list.

It wasn't that he disliked all teachers; Mr Starling, who read exciting stories and played brilliant football, he admired a lot. But Thomas and Mrs Twitchie had never cared for one another. They didn't like the look or the sound of each other at all. Nor did Thomas like her daughter, Gwendolyn, a nasty, squeaking sort of girl with yellow, corkscrew ringlets like worms. Yuck! And now Blossom's tennis ball lay in their garden, perhaps hiding behind a daffodil, or lying white – for it was a new, fluffy ball – and conspicuous in the middle of a freshly dug flowerbed.

Thomas walked on down the road, hands stuffed in his pockets, trying to look as if he hadn't just kicked a ball into Mrs Twitchie's garden. The street was quiet. No one stirred, not even a cat.

'I'll just leave it there,' he decided.

And yet . . . Blossom would make a hideous fuss if she missed it. She was like that, Thomas thought. Especially when it was something that she'd bought with her own pocket money.

Thomas halted, turned round and walked back. He stopped and stared dismally at the wall. The bricks glared back at him. One crooked one looked as if it was pulling faces at him, so Thomas poked his tongue out at it. Then he pushed the gate slightly with one hand. It swung open with a sinister grinding noise that made him shiver; like the creak of a dungeon door he thought.

Thomas stepped inside the garden and waited. No one was to be seen, and there was no sign of the Twitchie dog, a yappy beast called Jinxie. On tiptoe, and as one under a spell, Thomas moved silently forward and gazed at the green lawns and immaculate flowerbeds. There lay the tennis ball, looking like an overnight mushroom in the closely mown grass. Thomas peered nervously at the house itself. Everything was quiet, as deserted as the moon. Mrs Twitchie and Gwendolyn must have gone out, and there was no danger of Mr Twitchie appearing as he had left home some years ago. Life with Mrs Twitchie had proved too much for him, and he had departed one night in the middle of a thunderstorm.

Cautiously Thomas tiptoed along the path, with every nerve in his body screaming, 'Danger!' Peering left and then right, he stalked that ball like a cat after a nice fat thrush. The garden was still. He was perfectly safe. He'd just grab it and get away as fast as possible. Nearly there. His heart was beating loudly, but everything was all right. Now, over the flowerbed and on to the lawn, bend down, pick it up, and hooray! Next, escape.

Grrrrrrh, yap-yap. Grrrrrrh, yap-yap. Grrrrrrh, yap-yap. The silence was shattered as the Twitchie hound, a short-legged, motheaten terrier of ferocious disposition, bounced round the side of the house,

yapping, barking, growling, bouncing up and down like a rubber toy, eyes almost popping out of its head. It made angry runs and dashes at Thomas, who ran for the gate, the dog snatching and biting at his ankles.

'Mummy, Mummy!' There came a high-pitched shriek that he knew only too well. 'There's a boy in our garden. He might be a burgalar. Mummy, do come. Mummy! Mummy! Hurry up. It's terrible Thomas. It's Blossom's brother. Come and get him, Mummy!'

Pursued by the terrier and the yellow-haired

Gwendolyn, Thomas did his best to break the world speed record, and had almost reached the gate and safety when Mrs Twitchie came into view. At that moment the dog managed to get between him and his escape route and Thomas fell full length over it. The ball rolled into the road, and Gwendolyn, still calling 'Mummy', fell on top of Thomas.

'I've got him. Here he is, Mummy. Mummy, I've got him! He's kicking me! Horrible boy! Ow! Ow!'

Thomas tried to get up. The dog squirmed from under him and bounced and pounced all around him as he vainly tried to tear himself away from Gwendolyn's clutching fingers before Mrs Twitchie could seize him too. Other footsteps could now be heard as Mrs Twitchie hauled him to his feet, and Thomas, all hope gone, found he was gazing at the blue-clad form of PC Spriggs, an old enemy, who was saying, 'You in trouble again, eh? What is it this time?'

Mrs Twitchie answered for him, and, in a daze, Thomas heard that he had trespassed, caused a public disturbance, broken down a dozen daffodils, ruined a bed of tulips, kicked the dog and injured Gwendolyn's knee, causing it to bleed.

'I only went for my ball,' he protested. 'It didn't seem much . . .'

But PC Spriggs was much too busy talking himself to hear what Thomas was saying.

'Now, I'm going to warn you, you young hooligan, that you've got to stop this wild behaviour. Ruffians like you are ruining England today. What the world is coming to I don't know.'

He unbuttoned his pocket and fetched out his notebook.

'I'm going to put your name down in here, lad, and if I find you causing any more trouble this holiday, you'll be sorry, mark my words. Take that nasty look off your face and mark my words.'

Thomas nodded, trying hard to mark his words, whatever that meant. It was all too much for him. He just wanted to hide in a hole and cover himself with leaves, so that Mrs Twitchie, PC Spriggs and all the world would never find him.

'I think I'll just have a word with his mother,' the Constable continued.

'Thank you, Officer.' Mrs Twitchie smiled.

Sad at heart, Thomas set off, accompanied by the large figure in blue. He knew his mother would be angry and upset. So would Blossom, whose ball, the cause of all the trouble, had disappeared. Gwendolyn Twitchie was beaming joyously, patting Jinxie on the head, and Christopher Robin Baggs, and Lurcher Dench, more old enemies, had arrived just in time to see his progress home. Thomas felt terrible. His hands hurt where he had fallen over the dog and he tried to find a handkerchief to wrap round them, but, of course, he hadn't got one. Yuck!

They had nearly reached his house when a police Escort car drew up driven by PC Cubbins, as old a friend as PC Spriggs was an enemy. Crammed into the back seat, neat little trotters squashed under his enormous middle, was a huge, golden pig, a giant of a pig, the colour of beech leaves in autumn, with upstanding, furry ears and a long snout.

'Tamworth!' Thomas gasped in relief. 'Oh, Tamworth, I am pleased to see you.' Now everything would be all right. Tamworth Pig would solve any difficulties. Constable Cubbins opened the door and from the back seat of the car, which he completely filled, Tamworth emerged, panting like a large dog on a hot day.

'There's trouble up near Baggs's farm. Deadly Dench's motorbike gang are causing a rumpus. I think you'd better come along as well. Tamworth, 'ere, let me know,' PC Cubbins said.

'Yes, indeed. I think you're needed, Constable Spriggs. I'll look after Thomas.' Tamworth urged PC Spriggs firmly into the Escort as he spoke.

PC Cubbins slammed the door shut, crying, 'Let's get a move on,' and sped away before Constable Spriggs had had time to say anything at all.

'Thanks,' Thomas said to his friend. 'I thought I'd had it.'

'Always ready to help.' Tamworth grinned.

'Is Deadly really causing trouble?'

'Not much. But it'll keep Constable Spriggs happy. I saw Deadly, Constable Cubbins spotted you, so we got together, and here we are.' They beamed understandingly at one another.

A ball shot towards Thomas – Blossom's ball, kicked by Lurcher Dench, Deadly's brother, who was more a rival than an enemy.

'It's all yours,' he yelled.

'Thanks,' Thomas called back. The others turned

away, Christopher Robin scowling ferociously through his spots, and Gwendolyn drawing in her little mouth.

Thomas turned to his handsome, porky friend. 'Come back home with me,' Tamworth invited him.

Thomas climbed up on to the vast golden back, all cares forgotten. Sadness and bad luck were for other people, not for him.

'Giddy-up, Tamworth,' he cried and away they went.

Chapter Two

Above Pig House (Tamworth wouldn't ever call it a sty) grew his favourite damson tree, starry with spring blossom. The great pig loved all trees and had once successfully campaigned to save a nearby wood, called Tumbling Wood, from being torn up to make way for a motorway. Thomas and Blossom had helped him in this, as they had before on an earlier campaign to grow more food, or grub, as Thomas called it. Then Tamworth had been very busy organizing an anti-litter campaign.

Tamworth was now very famous, the President of the Animals' Union and the most important animal in Britain except for a certain racehorse and the Queen's corgies. Once a month he appeared on a television programme, where he interviewed other well-known personalities, such as the cats who eat the cat food on commercials, or winners of horse races. In his spare time he was writing the story of his life, which he was going to call 'A Pig's Tail' or 'The Tale of a Pig', he wasn't yet sure which. He was not very good with his trotters so Blossom was writing it down and illustrating it.

Thomas stayed under the damson tree talking to Tamworth until at last he said reluctantly that he ought to be going home. Tamworth walked with Thomas for part of the way. The night air was sharp and clear, and the stars shone in the sky.

'How peaceful it is,' Tamworth said. 'I think we're going to have a pleasant, quiet spring.'

When Thomas went to bed, Hedgecock and Mr Rab were awaiting him and quarrelling as usual. Hedgecock was a cantankerous beast with feathery prickles and a love of numbers. Mr Rab was long and thin, wore a striped red and white waistcoat and wrote poetry. They seldom agreed about anything.

'If you don't stop mumbling to yourself, I shall bash you. I suppose it's that rotten poetry.'

'I'm composing an epic poem.' Mr Rab spoke with dignity.

'What on earth's that when it's at home?'

'A long and grand poem.'

'Long and grand balderdash,' Hedgecock snorted, for he was a common animal. 'Why don't you do something useful, like learning to use a computer, for instance?' he continued.

'I don't think computers are any use AT ALL! The

world would be a much better place without them. Think of all those unhappy children at school being forced to learn about computers.' Mr Rab's voice rose higher and higher, ending in a loud shriek as Hedgecock kicked him.

'They like them, you stupid twit,' he grunted.

'I don't believe you.'

'You silly, striped thing. Why, we'd still be living in caves and up trees if it weren't for inventors and scientists and mathematicians, and *they* all use computers now,' Hedgecock went on.

'What does it matter where we live? The important thing is to spread love and beauty around us, like Blossom and I do,' Mr Rab said.

Hedgecock laughed so much that he fell off the bed and all his feathery prickles got ruffled.

'That serves you right,' Thomas said, scooping him off the floor. 'Get down to your place at the bottom of the bed. I'll ask you about maths next term. We've got a test when we go back.'

Hedgecock started to chant. 'A half is point five, a quarter is . . .'

'Oh, do shut up,' Mr Rab shrieked and Thomas threw the blanket of knitted squares over Hedgecock, the one that he loved to count. It took some minutes before the animal was able to struggle from under it, and then he settled into a cross, sulky heap, kicking out his legs from time to time.

Thomas got into bed and spread Num over him,
especially over his hands which were still sore. Num
was a soft, ragged piece of grey blanket, comforting
for sore places or when things went wrong. Thomas
did not like anyone to see Num.

Mr Rab warbled the Bedtime song very softly.
Thomas was really too old for it now, and he read a
book as Mr Rab sang, but part of him listened just the
same. Like Num, it was a great comfort, because they
had both been there as long as he could remember.
After a while he fell asleep on the book open on his
pillow and everything was at peace except for the
sound of Hedgecock snoring, wrapped in his blanket
of knitted squares.

Chapter Three

The end of term arrived at last, finishing with an assembly of the whole school in the last half-hour of the afternoon. The choir gathered on the platform together with the orchestra which Blossom had joined at the beginning of the year. Now she stood with the rest, holding her violin, looking incredibly stupid, thought Thomas. Lurcher Dench was gazing at her admiringly, for he had always liked Blossom. Thomas felt like kicking him as the choir and orchestra made their way through 'We're All Going to the Zoo'. It sounds as if the zoo's already here, Thomas thought.

Next, cycling proficiency awards were given out to those who'd passed the test and, after them, swimming awards. Blossom stepped forward for both, and then, finally, on her own to receive first prize for a painting competition that she'd entered. Thomas refused to clap or even to look. He stared at his feet, muttering all the worst words he could think of over and over again. He didn't want to see her receiving all this clapping and attention. It was all unfair. Didn't they realize how stupid she was?

Last of all, the children cheered the teachers and then Mrs Twitchie. Once again Thomas refused to join in. He was certainly *not* going to cheer Mrs Twitchie. What a perfectly dreadful day! He'd be pleased when it finished. Finally they left the hall and collected shoebags and the Easter cards they'd made. Once outside, Lurcher Dench kicked Thomas's card on to the ground. Thomas didn't mind as it was a hideous one – his Easter rabbit looked as if it had four ears and two legs – but it gave him an excuse to punch Lurcher. In a trice they were scuffling on the ground, pummelling one another, and Thomas suddenly felt much, much better. He liked scrapping with Lurcher. They battered and bashed each other happily, until they heard the irate voice of Mrs Twitchie and fled hastily.

Holidays, glorious holidays lay ahead. Great!

Easter came bringing with it the April rain, the sunshine and the flowers. Blossom took primroses and pussy willows to the Vicar's wife to decorate the church, and made an Easter garden with moss and leaves, tiny flowers and a round mirror for a pool.

Thomas, looking for an old lorry he'd lost, found it at the bottom of the dustbin bag he'd emptied everywhere. 'Yippee!' he cried, which isn't what his mother said when she found the rubbish. Thomas spent the rest of the day at Pig House.

Easter also brought Easter eggs. Blossom gazed with delight at hers, ignoring all Daddy's remarks about tooth decay, spots and fatness, to say nothing of wasted money. She didn't care. She stroked them all with careful fingers, and decided that she'd eat the one with the silver wrappings and the sugar violets first. But Thomas sold his to Christopher Robin Baggs, and bought a new football.

Easter also brought Great Aunt Hattie.

The children first heard about her when their mother, looking harassed, read out loud a letter to their father.

'. . . Cousin Winnie can't stand her a moment longer. She says that she will go dotty, too, and begs someone else to shoulder the burden for a while . . . Well, I expect we can manage the old lady.'

'Yes, but – Blossom, you're dropping jam everywhere. Do look what you're doing – where shall we put her?'

'In Thomas's room. He can share with Blossom. That's no problem,' said Mummy.

'I'm not going to sleep in that stupid girl's room. I want my own room,' Thomas shouted.

Blossom jumped out of her chair, and more jam fell on to the tablecloth.

'I don't want him in my room. He's horrible. He's mixed up all my paints because I won first prize and

16

he wasn't even mentioned. And he's jealous because I'm having a new bike and I'm older than he is and it's my turn first. That's fair.'

'It's not fair. It's not fair. Nothing's ever fair,' Thomas bawled at the top of his voice.

Daddy banged his fist down hard on the table and gave a loud roar. Tea flew all over the place, mostly over his toast.

'Given a straight choice, I'd rather eat with chimpanzees in a zoo than with you two. Now, sit down and listen. Great Aunt Hattie is coming to live with us for a while and you must behave yourselves and help to look after her. She's an old lady.'

'Who is she, anyway?' Blossom asked.

'She's my aunt, and so she's your great-aunt,' Daddy replied. 'You've met her before, a long time ago. She lived up north and then, when she got older, she went to stay with Cousin Winifred, but they haven't been getting on too well lately, and so she's coming to us for a time. And you will make her welcome!'

Daddy glared at Thomas, who said 'Yuck!' once too often and was sent upstairs, running fast in order to escape his father coming hard behind him. Safe in the room that he was soon to leave, he sat and brooded bitterly.

'What a life. What a miserable life. What with keeping out of old Spriggs's way and having to behave all the time because of this old girl who's coming, I might just as well be at school for all the fun I'll get.'

'If you're sorry, if you're sad, count your blessings and you'll be glad,' Mr Rab warbled, neck outstretched and nose a-quiver.

'What absolute rubbish!' Hedgecock shouted in his coarse voice. 'What's the point of counting blessings? First of all, with you around, I haven't got any, and second, the only things worth counting are numbers, glorious numbers.'

And he was off, counting away as fast as he could, until he fell suddenly asleep at number seven hundred and eighty-six.

Two days later, Great Aunt Hattie arrived. Daddy had gone to the station to meet her, and Blossom, Thomas and their mother were waiting in the hall. It seemed a long time, but at last the car drew up and out scrambled a very little lady, all in black, wearing a flat hat skewered with three huge pins. In one hand she carried an enormous paper carrier bag, and in the other a large basket from which emerged a blood-curdling yowling. Behind her staggered Daddy, bearing three suitcases, two cardboard boxes and a hat box – Blossom and Thomas had never seen one of these before, and they only found out what it was later.

'She looks like the grandmothers you see in

cartoons,' Blossom said.

'I'm off,' Thomas muttered, moving very fast.

But his mother grabbed him. 'Oh no, you're staying right here to say hello.'

The old lady surveyed them through sharp eyes surrounded by crinkles. 'You're all here, then. Good, good, good. It's nice to see you again, Miriam,' she said, pecking Mummy's cheek.

19

'I'm not Miriam,' Mummy said gently.

'No, no, of course not. And this is, what do you call her? Blossom? Stupid name. I shall call you Jane. Jane is plain and suitable.'

'I don't like . . .' Blossom began, but her great-aunt was not listening. She was speaking to Thomas.

'Ah, you look troublesome, boy. Exactly like my brother Ted, the one who ran away to sea. Are you troublesome, boy?'

'No,' Thomas replied. 'Have you brought a present? And what's in that?' He pointed to the noisy basket, that rocked with feline rage.

'That's my little pussy cat, Vespa. Yes, you've all got presents. In my big bag. But first we must let out dear Puss. He's in a wicked temper.'

This was evidently true, to judge from the spitting and swearing coming from the basket, to say nothing of the spiked, curving claws that protruded from a hole in the top.

'On guard,' Great Aunt Hattie cried, and with a swift motion opened the basket. A furry mass spilt out and, howling horribly, fled to the kitchen, followed by the old lady.

'Butter his paws,' she screamed. 'Butter his paws.'

'Whatever for?' cried Blossom, running behind, followed by her mother.

'To make him stay, of course, Jane. By the time he's

licked all the butter off, he'll be ready to settle down.'

'Don't try too hard,' said Daddy, not a great cat lover. Besides, he was carrying a vast amount of luggage upstairs.

Vespa retired to a large cooking bowl on a high shelf and crouched there, spitting and defying all comers.

'He likes it there,' said Great Aunt Hattie. 'He'll be all right.'

'You could've fooled me,' said Thomas.

'But it's my cooking basin,' Mummy protested. 'I don't want cat hairs in it.'

'Don't be unreasonable, Miriam. Just be grateful it's not your best hat.'

'I don't wear hats,' Mummy replied coldly. She didn't like being called Miriam. But Great Aunt Hattie was looking around.

'Where's that boy, James?'

'I'm called Thomas.'

'Such nonsense, when you're the spitting image of your Uncle James.'

'But you said he looked like Ted, the one who ran away to sea,' cried Blossom, by now thoroughly bewildered.

'Rubbish, Jane. I said nothing of the kind.'

Blossom opened her mouth to protest and then closed it again. As far as she could see Great Aunt Hattie was completely barmy.

'Now, James, you butter his paws, while Miriam makes me a nice cup of tea.'

'She's not called Miriam,' Blossom sighed, but her great-aunt was suddenly looking all about her.

'Where's my bag? Where's it gone? All the presents are in it. James, where's my bag?'

'I took all your belongings upstairs,' Daddy said quietly. 'And he really is called Thomas.'

'You can fetch it, then, boy. Why on earth did you let them give you all those names, Thomas, James, Ted? You ought to settle for one of them, you know, boy.'

'I'll settle for Thomas,' said the boy, grinning.

Great Aunt Hattie waved a black-clad arm. 'Come on, let's have our tea and open the presents all together. Come along. Don't mess about.'

The carrier bag was full of unexpected shapes and lumps. Great Aunt Hattie was no neat wrapper of parcels. Some were in brown paper tied up with string, while others were wrapped in newspaper. Thomas and Blossom, Mummy and Daddy sat and waited while Great Aunt Hattie felt all around the parcels, nodding to herself at intervals. She noisily drank up her tea and settled back her false teeth which were wobbling up and down. Thomas liked this.

'Cousin Winifred sends her love. She's going to plant tomatoes this year, she says, because of the price of food.'

'Aren't you going to open the presents?' Blossom asked, for the suspense was terrible.

'Who cares what Cousin Winifred is planting?' Thomas cried.

'Don't be rude, James. Cousin Winifred is a very worthy, if rather dull, woman. I don't think you should mock her.'

'I wasn't mocking. I just want to see what you've brought me.'

In answer, Great Aunt Hattie slowly drew not one but three pins out of her hat. They were enormous, long things, with bobbles on the end, one silver, one gold and one turquoise. She stuck them in the arm of her chair. Mummy, with a shiver, removed them to a safe place. Then Great Aunt Hattie took off her hat. Underneath it her hair was a rich, bright brown.

It's a wig, thought Daddy, Mummy and Blossom simultaneously. Thomas didn't notice. He was too busy looking at the presents. As quick as lightning, Great Aunt Hattie had up-ended the bag on to the floor, then started tearing off the wrappings and running round to each person – for you – and you – and you. When she'd finished she sat back triumphantly, smiling broadly, as Daddy, Mummy, Blossom and Thomas stared at each other over an extraordinary collection of objects.

Mummy had a cactus plant, a new duster, an ancient pewter shoe, a card of buttons, a bag of mushrooms, a tin of sardines and a paperback book with a grisly corpse on the front.

Blossom had a red hot-water bottle, an enormous lollipop, a reel of blue cotton, a pink comb, a velvet hair ribbon, and a blow-up rubber toy which turned out to be a ladybird when it was inflated.

For Daddy there was a portrait of Winston Churchill, a car shampoo, a box of matches, a tin of soup, a can of beer and a ballpoint pen.

Thomas was given a calendar with some months missing, a packet of dried peas, a rubber ball, a ruler, a stuffed frog, the largest bar of chocolate he had ever seen, and a sword in a scabbard.

The old lady peered into their faces, then clapped her hands as they looked in surprise at all the presents.

'I don't know what to say,' Mummy said at last.

'I do.' Blossom went up to the old lady, put her arms round her and kissed her. 'Welcome,' she said.

Chapter Four

Tamworth Pig sat reading a letter he had received
that morning. He wore a pair of spectacles on his
snout. They had thick, black frames and he liked
them very much. Melanie thought how handsome
and clever he looked, but then, she always did. He
sat in the corner in his big rocking chair, given to him
for his work for the environment. The chair was
made of dark, polished wood, with a red velvet
cushion, and it rocked away very smoothly.
Suddenly there was a knock on the door and
Thomas, Blossom and Great Aunt Hattie walked in.

'I've so wanted to meet you,' cried Great Aunt
Hattie, advancing on Tamworth, who stood up
courteously. He extended his right front trotter and
she shook it up and down, up and down, like a pump
handle.

'I must say how much I admire your work,' Great
Aunt Hattie went on. 'And I'm anxious to know what
your next cause is going to be.'

'Just now, I'm taking it easy, and enjoying staying
at home,' replied Tamworth.

Great Aunt Hattie fidgeted with excitement. She
bobbed up and down and then took the three hatpins
out of her hat, and took it off. She put the pins down
on Tamworth's transistor radio, where Blossom
watched them, fascinated.

'I think,' said the old lady, and she clapped her
hands, 'I think it should be . . . BRING BACK
BIKES!'

'But they've never gone,' Thomas said bitterly,
'and I know because *she's*' – he pointed a downward
thumb at Blossom – 'going to have a new one next
week because *she's* passed her cycling proficiency

test. I shan't get one for ages. All I've got is a mouldy old secondhand one, not fit for the rubbish dump. I've had it for years and years and years and my knees get stuck. It's not fair.'

He fell into one of his black moods.

'It's not my fault,' Blossom retorted. 'You'll get yours in time. I can't help being older than you.'

Great Aunt Hattie broke in impatiently. 'Yes, I know, lots of children ride bikes, but thousands of grown-ups don't. They're the ones I want to appeal to.' She stopped abruptly. 'Oh, by the way, Tamworth, I've brought you a cabbage,' she said, reaching out for a large paper bag. 'Especially grown by Cousin Winifred. She grows fine cabbages herself, even if she is an extremely dull woman. As a matter of fact, she's a bit like a cabbage.' She thought about this for a moment, and then dipped in her bag again. 'Here's a mirror for you, Melanie, so that you can see how pretty you are.'

'What do you think of my idea then?' the old lady went on. 'About bikes?'

'It's an excellent one,' the pig agreed. 'But I'm really not undertaking anything new at present. I fancy a holiday. But that's no reason why you shouldn't take it up. I'm sure you'd get a lot of support. And Thomas and Blossom will help you with posters and I know lots of pigeons who are

28

happy to deliver leaflets.'

But Blossom and Thomas were both so busy playing that they didn't really hear, and Thomas was not at all interested in saving bikes anyway.

Hedgecock began to speak the moment Thomas went into the bedroom that night. 'I've never agreed with old pink-nose, here, before,' he growled as Thomas climbed into bed. 'But we're telling you, both of us, together . . .'

'Yes, both of us, together,' squeaked Mr Rab.

'Shut up and let me get on with it. What I'm saying is that we're both fed up . . .'

'Upset and unhappy.'

'Life's not worth living . . .'

'If it goes on like this, I shall go and live with my friend the Welsh Rabbit, in the Tumbling Wood.'

'Would you really?' Hedgecock asked. 'Well, that makes it all a bit different. In that case . . .'

'You shouldn't say things like that. You know how lonely you'd be without me,' squeaked the indignant rabbit.

'I'd learn to manage all right.'

Mr Rab burst into tears.

'Oh shut up, you stripey fool. I didn't mean it,' Hedgecock growled.

Thomas interrupted them. 'Just a minute. I don't

29

know what you're talking about. Tell me what's the matter.'

'It's that cat,' they said together, and light dawned on Thomas.

'Oh, Vespa, you mean.'

'Yes. Him. And something else is wrong too. It's bad enough not sleeping in our own room, with all our things, but your mother has put my blanket of knitted squares on your great-aunt's bed. She's as mad as a hatter anyway. Not that that worries me. All your mad great-aunts can come and live with you as far as I'm concerned. *But I want my blanket back.* I can't get to sleep properly unless I've counted my squares.' Hedgecock stopped, out of breath.

'Oh, that's why I haven't heard you snoring lately, is it?' asked Mr Rab.

Hedgecock glared at him furiously. 'I – do – not – snore,' he said through his teeth.

'Yes, you do, just like a million bumblebees on a summer day in a beanfield. Don't hit me. Ow! Oowwh!'

Hedgecock didn't hit him. He kicked him very hard instead, right out of the bed. Mr Rab lay in a crumpled heap on the floor.

Thomas picked up the sad little fellow and snuggled him under Num.

'I thought you two were supposed to be agreeing. It doesn't seem like it.'

'We are agreeing. That is, provided he says that I don't snore.'

'You don't snore,' Mr Rab sniffed, wiping his eyes with Num. 'And now I'm telling a lie and Blossom doesn't like me telling lies . . .' He sobbed even louder.

'Oh shut up,' Thomas commanded, for he was not patient by nature, and he felt he'd heard enough of Mr Rab's sorrows. 'Get on with telling me about the cat. You haven't said anything about him yet.'

'He's a beast.'

'A monster.'

'A fiend.'

'He's horrible,' they chorused together.

'But what's he done to you?'

Mr Rab wrapped his thin arms round himself and shivered.

Hedgecock sighed deeply and began. 'It was all right at first. He stayed in that basin of your mother's for ages, until he got used to it here, then he started creeping and sneaking over the house. And he took to coming in here the minute you'd gone out, sitting himself on that window sill, and watching the birds to try and catch them, though they're too clever for him, mostly, and it was then he started to say the horrible things.'

'What things?'

Mr Rab went on in his quavering voice. 'He kept

saying how funny-looking and silly we were, and
that he'd never met anyone as pathetic as us in all his
life – '

'*Us*,' Hedgecock interrupted furiously. '*Us!
Pathetic!* Me with my marvellous maths and Mr Rab
with his beautiful poetry.'

'Oh, oh! Hedgecock!' cried Mr Rab.

It was the first time Hedgecock had ever said
anything polite about Mr Rab's poetry.

'Well, you shouldn't take any notice of that,' said
Thomas; 'I say things like that to Christopher Robin
Baggs all the time. Because in his case, it's true.'

'But you see' – Mr Rab's voice quavered up and
down furiously – 'that's not all . . .' He paused, pink
nose quivering like mad.

'Well, come on.'

'He says we're no . . . not . . . real. Not real. Oh, Thomas!'

Mr Rab howled and Hedgecock counted up to a hundred very rapidly to stop himself doing the same. Thomas took Num and wrapped it carefully round both his friends.

'Don't you worry,' he said. 'I'll fix that cat. And I'll get the blanket back. In fact, I'll get it now.'

He padded away and returned with it in a jiffy. He put it at the bottom of the bed and Hedgecock shot down to it, counting very fast.

'Now, sleep,' Thomas ordered. 'And don't worry. Sing the Bedtime song, Mr Rab.'

> 'Mr Rab has gone to sleep
> Tucked in his tiny bed,
> He has curled up his little paws
> And laid down his sleepy head.'

When he'd finished Mr Rab asked quietly, 'Are we real, Thomas?'

'Of course, you are. To me, anyway,' said Thomas.

Chapter Five

Blossom's new bike arrived after Easter and sent
Thomas into the deepest of glooms. The unfairness of
life was just too much. Moodily he surveyed his small
and battered bike, with its bent handlebars and its
rusty wheels, and his heart was as heavy as lead.
Blossom's bicycle was blue, with a white saddle and a
bag on the back. It gleamed and shone and sparkled
in the sunlight as Blossom, showing off all the skills
she'd acquired in her cycling proficiency lessons,
rode up and down, watched by Gwendolyn Twitchie,
Lurcher Dench and Christopher Robin Baggs, all
admiring her.

Thomas watched for a moment, then strode darkly
away, feeling sick inside. He took his father's
hammer out of the toolbox, and walked up to his old,
small, battered bike. Lifting the hammer, he bashed
the bike carefully and thoroughly until the ground
was covered with metal bits. Then he stalked upstairs
and threw himself on his bed, ignoring Mr Rab and
Hedgecock, who tried vainly to comfort him. He
knew he would be in trouble but he didn't care, for he

didn't care about anything at all. The spring sun
shone through the bedroom window, and he could
hear the voices of the children outside, cycling up
and down. They were laughing in the sunshine, but
Thomas's thoughts were as cold as a winter night.

From downstairs came the sound of Great Aunt
Hattie's voice. 'You should have given James one as
well. I know how I would feel. Furious.'

35

His mother answered. 'Thomas has only to wait a little while. Bikes are expensive and he will get one in his turn. I don't think he should make such a fuss.'

'Grown-ups never understand,' Thomas whispered to Hedgecock and Mr Rab. 'I know Dad won't when he finds out what I've done. But I don't care.'

However, he did care when Daddy not only stopped a week's pocket money but made him tidy up all the mess he'd made. It took ages and his father kept talking about behaviour and goodness and so on. Life seemed very hard.

But Blossom gave him half her pocket money and offered him a ride on the new bike. The money he accepted, but not the ride. He wanted nothing at all to do with her machine.

Chapter Six

Thomas's misery continued. Blossom was now out every day riding her bike, and, after a time, going on longer trips with Lurcher Dench, who accompanied her faithfully on the most clapped-out vehicle ever seen, held together with string. Yet he managed to go much faster on it than ever Christopher Robin Baggs did on his brand-new, bright red machine, or Gwendolyn Twitchie on her elegant green one on which she was not allowed to get a speck of mud or Mummy would be cross, so she spent most of her time polishing it with the collection of dusters she kept in the saddlebag. In any case, Gwendolyn was very wobbly, and afraid to go far. So Blossom and Lurcher went further and further afield on their own.

Thomas was jealous. He skulked and scowled and called Lurcher names when he saw him. But he couldn't fight him properly because Lurcher got away so speedily on his ancient jet bike as he called it.

For a while football games with his friend Henry helped, but then came the final blow. Henry announced that the football season was definitely

over for that year, and next day he too turned out
with Blossom and Lurcher, happily riding a bike
almost as antique as Lurcher's. Now Thomas wished
he hadn't wrecked his old machine, for he could have
cycled round with the others. So he turned on
Christopher Robin, who was having difficulty in
starting, pulled him off and kicked his bike now lying
on the ground. And walked straight into the
protruding middle of PC Spriggs.

This time there was no PC Cubbins, nor any great
golden pig to save him. Thomas was all on his own as
he was marched along to the Baggs's farmhouse,
wheeling Christopher Robin's hated bicycle. Mrs
Baggs put on her best nylon overall, covered with
purple pansies, and came to see Thomas's mother, to
whom she said a great many dreadful things, some of
which were true. When Daddy came home, the
whole business had to be gone through again while
Thomas sat as though turned to stone. Blossom tried
to speak up for him, but was told not to interfere. She
crept up to bed. Daddy in a rage was bad enough, but
Daddy cold and icy was the end.

At last Thomas went to bed too, and lay curled
under Num, not speaking, not crying. Mr Rab put
out a thin paw to touch him, but it was shrugged
away, and the Bedtime song was not sung. Blossom
came over to his bed, but he pushed her away too.

Sometime in the middle of the night, when Thomas had woken up for the fiftieth time, he heard a noise by his bedside. Opening his eyes, he felt afraid, wondering what it was, for it looked like a weird, old ghost. His heart bumped pit-pat pit-pat until the ghost spoke.

'Here, James. Cheer up. You're very like your Great Uncle Ted, and he was always in trouble. Have some of this.'

Into Thomas's hand was pushed what seemed to be the biggest bar of chocolate he had ever received, bigger even than the one Great Aunt Hattie had given to him on the day she arrived, and exactly what his mother disapproved of.

He peeled back the wrapping thankfully, for he had had no tea. It tasted fantastic.

'Shh . . . don't wake the girl, what's her name? And listen to me, boy. You've been making a right mess of things as far as I can see. But I think you're sorry now. Are you sorry, boy?'

The boy nodded in the darkness.

'Well, Tamworth and I have been having a little talk, and we've got an idea. Now, go to sleep, and in the morning go to see Tamworth, a clever pig, that one.'

'Oh yes. He'll help me,' Thomas whispered, and fell asleep immediately. He did not even hear Great Aunt Hattie go out of the room.

Next morning he awoke feeling better than he had for days.

'And about time, too,' Hedgecock told him. 'You've done nothing about that cat and it's pestering the life out of us. Stop thinking about yourself and be nice to all of us and then everything will seem better.'

'Hark who's talking! You've never been nice to anyone in your life, least of all me,' Mr Rab cried.

Hedgecock hit him, just to prove him wrong.

'There, you see what I mean,' sniffed Mr Rab.

Hedgecock pushed him off the bed.

Into the cool morning ran Thomas, his friends behind him panting breathlessly, trying to keep up with him, Thomas running like the wind at the thought of seeing Tamworth once more. He reached Pig House, pushed open the door and flung himself on to the immense pig, who awoke with a start as Thomas snuggled into the red-gold side.

'Oh, Tamworth, it's a wonderful world,' Thomas cried, rolling over and over.

'I suppose it is for those who like waking up early. I've always found sleep quite delightful, myself.' Tamworth yawned, stretching himself from the tips of his ears to his tiny trotters and furry tail, so that he rippled all over like a field of wheat in the breeze. Then, slowly, he heaved himself to his trotters.

'There's something for you behind Pig House,' he said. 'Your great-aunt has been extremely active on your behalf. This is very kind of her, for your behaviour has been bad, I hear. Stop blowing down my ears, impertinent boy.'

In reply, Thomas climbed on Tamworth's back to go out of the door, holding tight to the funny golden ears, Hedgecock and Mr Rab clinging on behind.

'Let's go, Thomas,' Tamworth said.

They went round to the back of the Pig House where the lean-to seemed to have been transformed into an ironmongery shop, for there were odd pieces of metal everywhere. In the middle of it all stood two very old bicycles, without tyres.

'I know they don't look much at the moment,' said Tamworth, 'but a good friend of mine is coming this

morning with new tyres, and spare bits and pieces.
He's an excellent mechanic, and the bikes should be
quite safe and roadworthy when he's finished with
them. Then you and I can paint them, Thomas, that
is, if you will allow me to help you, dear boy, for
although I'm not proficient at painting, I do enjoy it
greatly.'

Thomas slid off Tamworth's back and investigated the two machines.

'Oh yes, they'll be really brill. I'll have that one. We'll make it look super. It's the right size for me, and it's miles better than old Lurcher Dench's. But, whose is this one? Yours?'

'No, that's for your Great Aunt Hattie. She picked them up at the scrapyard, and when hers has been done up and painted, she's going to learn to ride it, she says.'

'Coo! That should be interesting. But when's this mechanic coming?'

'Fred? Oh, he'll be here about ten o'clock. Come along when you've had your breakfast and see what he does. Which reminds me, I must go and see what breakfast I am to be presented with this morning. It's greatly improved, you know, since Farmer Baggs brings it instead of Mrs Baggs.'

'Why did she stop coming?'

'She tripped one day, and fell in a bucket of old cabbage leaves and potato peelings, so she refused to come ever again. I was terribly upset, as you can imagine.'

Tamworth went in and Thomas turned for home, promising to return at ten.

Once back in the house he decided to settle with Great Aunt Hattie's cat, but Vespa was nowhere to be found, though Thomas searched everywhere.

'Never mind, I'll deal with him,' Thomas promised his friends.

During the following days, which were also the last remaining ones of the holiday, Thomas worked away at the bike, together with Fred, Tamworth and Great Aunt Hattie. She had chosen purple with silver stars for her machine, while Thomas thought that red would be best. They oiled, rubbed down, fitted new brakes and lamps and tyres. Finally Fred pronounced the bikes to be in first-class working order. Thomas was so busy that he didn't have time to be miserable or to worry about going back to school. All was peace. Hedgecock and Mr Rab were their old selves now that Vespa had disappeared, though Great Aunt Hattie still ran up and down the garden path calling, 'Puss, puss, puss,' every evening.

Tamworth was especially contented. He loved painting. His trotters were awkward and he always finished the day covered in paint, but he said happily, 'I do like a quiet life. This suits me very well. Sometimes I think I shall give up my public work and become a decorator or perhaps a farmer.'

'I don't think that you would be the same pig without your causes,' Melanie remarked.

'Perhaps you're right. Nevertheless, I've decided upon one thing.'

'What's that?' asked Thomas.

'When Great Aunt Hattie has learnt to ride, then *I* shall have a go.'

'You'll need a giant model, specially reinforced.' Thomas grinned, and Tamworth knocked him head over heels with his snout, for impertinence.

Thomas's bike was ready first, for he only had to paint two coats of red, whereas Great Aunt Hattie had to wait for her purple coat to dry before she could apply the stars. Accompanied by Tamworth, Thomas practised for a while near Pig House until he felt confident, then sailed triumphantly towards the

group of children with their bicycles, among whom was Blossom. Cries and shouts greeted him as he circled in beside Henry.

'Where are we off to this afternoon, then? Let's go somewhere interesting, because it's school tomorrow and we might as well make the most of today.'

'I know,' Blossom cried. 'I'll go and get some food while you all decide where we're going.'

Food always played a very important part in anything Blossom did. No outing was complete without food.

'Suppose we ride along that track where the railway lines have been taken up. There's no traffic,' Henry suggested.

'Yeah. We can have races there. I'll beat you, Measlebug,' Lurcher challenged.

'You've had more practice than me,' Thomas shouted.

'Whose's fault's that, then?'

It could have turned into their usual battle, but at that moment Blossom returned with various packages, murmuring to herself, 'Crisps and cheese sandwiches and bananas and apples and coke. It should be enough, I hope.'

Then she went back for some more.

'Mummy says I can't come,' Gwendolyn Twitchie said, appearing among them.

'Nobody asked you, anyway,' snapped Lurcher

Dench, who mostly talked like Hedgecock.

'Where's Baggsy?' Thomas asked as they set off.

'Well may you ask,' Henry answered. 'After you had laid him and his bicycle flat, Mummy Baggs sent him for a holiday away from these nasty rough boys round here. You, in fact. And he's not coming back till next week.'

'Good,' Thomas shouted. 'Come on, Lurcher.'

Soon they reached the old forsaken railway track that always made Tamworth sad when he saw it, for he was a great train lover and missed them not running any more. There Lurcher beat Thomas in a race, but not by much, so he intended to win next time. Then they had a picnic sitting on the old dilapidated seat, still standing outside the deserted station whose windows had all been boarded up and where the weeds and the willowherb sprawled wildly.

In bed that night Mr Rab said, 'You know we haven't seen that diabolical cat for ages.'

'That's not a word,' Hedgecock sniffed.

'Yes, it is. Diabolical means devilish or fiendish.'

'All these stupid, long-winded words are a load of rubbish. What *is* important is that that horrible animal seems to have gone, thank goodness.'

Hedgecock settled himself comfortably in his squared blanket at the bottom of the bed as Thomas wrapped Num round Mr Rab and himself.

Hedgecock looked up after a time, eyes bright. 'What a good thing it is that you are going back to school. We can do some more maths and go through all those beautiful tables.'

'Oh no!' squeaked Mr Rab.

But Hedgecock started to recite happily, falling suddenly asleep when he reached five times thirteen.

Chapter Seven

School wasn't too bad. Thomas had a seat by Henry, started French, began a project on pond life, and played his first game of cricket that season. He was also told off by Mrs Twitchie on three separate occasions.

Daddy had been pleased about the bicycle, and grinned when Thomas grunted that he was sorry about breaking up the other one. Daddy thought the new machine was excellent, admired the paintwork, and said that he thought Thomas ought to take the cycling proficiency course that term, whereupon Great Aunt Hattie said that she wanted to do it too. And off she pottered to see Mr Spokewheel, who was in charge of the course, and he agreed that she should join the children on Thursday, after school.

The following Thursday saw a line-up of boys and girls with their bikes, about twenty of them, including Thomas and Christopher Robin Baggs, and, among them, the small figure of Great Aunt Hattie with her purple and silver machine. For the occasion she was wearing a pair of long, voluminous trousers with elastic at the bottom, called bloomers, left over, she said, from the days when she had cycled before, for a short while.

'That was before the first Great War,' she said.

'Goodness me!' Blossom exclaimed.

'Did you live in a cave when you were young?' asked Thomas.

The only person not happy was Mummy. She went to have a word privately with Mr Spokewheel, to ask him to take care of the old lady. Great Aunt Hattie would have been furious if she'd known.

At last they were all ready with Great Aunt Hattie last in line, singing, 'Down at the Old Bull and Bush' to herself, making Thomas a bit embarrassed. She sang continually, mostly hymns and old music-hall songs.

Mr Spokewheel had placed small white cube blocks in carefully spaced lines, and the children had to ride round them without touching one, which required good control and steering. Then they had to pull up quickly at a tape held by Blossom and Gwendolyn Twitchie, to show that their brakes were in full working order and that they knew how to use them.

Most of the children had done a fair amount of riding and found it quite simple. Thomas did his round without making a mistake, then sat back to watch Great Aunt Hattie.

At last her turn came and she wheeled her bike

forward. It looked too big for her, as it was one of the old-fashioned high ones and she had short legs. Mr Spokewheel held it for her while she struggled on to the seat. Thomas saw that his mother was watching with her friends Mrs Postlewaithe and the Vicar's wife. Her face was pale and she looked anxious, and Thomas realized, suddenly, that he was worried too. He looked at his great-aunt and decided that he'd look after her if he had to. But Mr Spokewheel was holding her steady.

'Don't bother with the blocks. Just steer straight for the tape, put your brakes on and dismount, and that will be enough for today.'

Great Aunt Hattie patted her hat with a terrified yet determined hand, then gripped both handlebars tightly and pushed hard on the pedals. Away she shot, like a greyhound out of the trap, released after the hare. Pedalling like mad, she shot through the blocks and headed for the tape. The girls dropped it quickly and leapt out of the way.

'Slow down!' bellowed Mr Spokewheel.

'I can't,' she yelled back, her little legs in the old-fashioned bloomers going round like pistons.

'I knew it! I knew it!' cried Mummy, rushing into the school playground towards her aunt.

'Look out,' Great Aunt Hattie bawled, as they headed for each other.

'Mummy! Mummy!' Blossom screamed.

Her mother just managed to jump out of the path of the oncoming machine as the old lady roared through the open gate and on to the main road, where the afternoon traffic was building up fast. Mr Spokewheel seized the nearest child's machine, jumped on it and went after her. Unfortunately he was a tall man, with long legs, and he'd grabbed the smallest bike in the playground, so he had to cycle with his knees very wide apart to avoid hitting the handlebars. Thomas, too, now aware of the danger, shot forward like an arrow from a bow, and tore after his Great Aunt Hattie, followed by the other children.

'They'll all be killed,' screeched the Vicar's wife, her powerful voice rising like a fire-engine warning. 'Look out! Look out! Danger!'

She ran into the middle of the road, where three cars narrowly missed her, and started to haul off her clothes.

'What on earth are you doing?' Mummy cried despairingly, rushing after her.

'Red petticoat. To stop the cars. Like the Railway Children.'

By now she had torn off her red petticoat and was flapping it up and down, like a matador at a bull fight, shouting 'Stop!' at the top of her voice. Traffic braked noisily to a stop as ordered.

But Great Aunt Hattie was by now far ahead, a downhill slope accelerating her already tremendous pace. Round a lorry she swerved, missing a bus by inches, then passing one of the local leather jackets on his motorbike as if he were standing still. He left the gang some time later and was never the same again.

'Stop her! Try to stop her!' beseeched Mr Spokewheel as he flew past pedestrians, while behind him pedalled the entire cycling proficiency class, streaming along like bees swarming.

Yet nothing could stop Great Aunt Hattie now. All fear had left her and she knew only the exhilarating thrill of speed. The wind whistled round her face. Her hat had blown off long ago, despite its hatpins. She felt like some god riding the mountain tops, an eagle plunging from a snowy crest, a rocket zooming to the furthest stars. Faster she went, and still faster. Faster, she thought, than anyone had ever gone before. She was breaking the world speed record, going through the sound barrier, travelling faster than the speed of light. She saw no danger; she could imagine no danger, as the hill sent her on at a terrific pace. Hands gripping the handlebars, bloomers flapping in the breeze, little legs a blur, on flew Great Aunt Hattie.

Then, out of the blue, a gigantic juggernaut, came towards her, filling the road as it overtook a car.

And terrible fear fell on Great Aunt Hattie.

She could not see how she could possibly miss it.

On and on they came, the juggernaut and Great Aunt Hattie. She couldn't cry out. Filled with terror, she thought: This is it.

Then, flashing up on the left, appeared a narrow turning leading to Baggs's farm and Pig House.

Somehow she wrenched the handlebars over and turned into the lane, where she began to slow down, for it sloped gently uphill. And there, taking a pleasant stroll, were Melanie and Tamworth Pig.

'I can't stop,' yelled the old lady.

Tamworth summed up the situation in a second. Turning so that he was broadside on to her (and in his case the side was extremely broad), despite the fact that he had once been hit by a motorbike and it had hurt, he stood quite still with Melanie quivering a bit beside him.

'Squeeze both hands hard underneath on the brakes,' he cried.

Knowing at last what to do, she squeezed hard. The bike came to a shuddering halt and fell over. Great Aunt Hattie catapulted in a flying heap on to Tamworth, who rocked on his trotters but remained upright as she slid unharmed to the road, where she sat, looking dazed, murmuring as she did so, 'Wonderful. Super. Absolutely super-duper wonderful.'

She was still saying this over and over again, as Mr Spokewheel, Thomas, the cycling proficiency class, various interested spectators, Mummy, Blossom, the Vicar's wife and Mrs Postlewaithe all arrived, Mummy frantic. Blossom picked up the ancient machine and wheeled it back. It was quite undamaged. The children were sent home, told that they'd had sufficient proficient riding for that day, and a lift back was given to Great Aunt Hattie, who sat in the front of the car, still saying, 'Absolutely super-duper wonderful,' at intervals.

'I do see what Cousin Winifred meant. She's absolutely batty, you know,' Mummy said to Daddy, that night.

'Mm. I think you're right. By the way, that cat of hers is back. I think it's been out on the tiles, for it's all bedraggled. But if it gets on my lettuces again, there'll be trouble.'

On her way to bed, Blossom popped in to see Great Aunt Hattie who had gone to bed early after her exciting ride. So had Mummy, to keep up her strength, she said. When Blossom entered, the old lady was propped up on four pillows because she didn't like lying flat. Her feet didn't reach far down the bed and she looked pale.

'Find my spectacles for me, dear,' she said. 'I feel like reading in bed and I can't remember where I put them.'

Blossom searched and searched but could not see them. Finally she looked at her great-aunt. 'Why, there they are on your nose,' she cried.

Great Aunt Hattie felt her nose. 'So they are. Fancy that, my dear.'

Blossom sat down on the patchwork cover that the old lady had brought with her. She stroked and admired it, while Great Aunt Hattie told her about the hexagons of material, how old they were and when they had first been used. One piece of sprigged flannelette was the same as her high-necked nightgown, which Blossom thought was beautiful. Next she went on to admire the collection of ornaments on the dressing table: little china shoes, a china tree for hanging rings on, and a heart-shaped red velvet pincushion for sticking her eighteen hatpins in.

'All these things are nice, but they don't look right in here, not with Thomas's football pictures on the wall and all his comics over there in the corner,' Blossom said.

'Oh, but I like those. I read them before I go to sleep. I do get bored with old-fashioned things, you know, and I like football.'

'Still, if you moved in with me, instead of Thomas, I could look at all your lovely things and talk to you, instead of listening to his grumbling and having him mess up all my stuff.'

Great Aunt Hattie agreed, so Thomas moved back to his own room, and she went into Blossom's. Hedgecock was delighted.

But Vespa soon found them. The fiendish cat sat there, grooming himself, very noisily, yawning at intervals.

'I've had a simply splendid time,' he purred. 'That vicarage pussy is a little smasher. But now I need a meal, a wash and a sleep, so I'll see you later, you poor, stuffed things.'

And he was gone, before they could think up a reply.

Chapter Eight

During May Tamworth Pig was summoned urgently to a large town where there was a threat to tear up a beautiful valley, full of flowers and trees and animals, in order to fill it up with rubble and build a car park there. Many people in that town, horrified at this idea, had drawn up a petition with five thousand names on it, asking if the car park could be made elsewhere, if it were indeed necessary that it should be built at all. And these people had asked Tamworth to go and speak at a meeting, because of his work in saving trees, for their valley was full of fine trees. Many grown-ups and children turned up at the meeting, and the giant pig was met by clapping and loud cheering when he stepped on to the platform to make his speech.

He spoke rousingly and was warmly applauded, so, after several invitations, he decided to stay there for a few days, and see if he could save the valley for all time. Furthermore, he had been invited to a banquet where thirty different types of cabbages and greens were to be offered to him and Tamworth could

not resist the sheer delight of this.

Actually he spoke so well and worked so hard that it was declared that no one should ever build on the valley, and the rabbits and birds, the children and the old people would be able to enjoy its peace and beauty for ever.

Meanwhile, back at home, Great Aunt Hattie was progressing with her campaign. Blossom designed some posters saying 'BRING BACK BIKES' and 'BICYCLES ARE BEAUTIFUL'. Great Aunt Hattie nailed a handle to a board and stuck one of the posters to it, rather messily, Blossom thought, but did not say so. Blossom's mother was not too pleased about the whole business.

'I don't want her to be involved with bicycles,' she said quietly to Blossom. 'I still haven't recovered from that nightmare ride of hers. I was sure she'd be killed.'

But surprisingly enough, when Great Aunt Hattie turned up for the next cycling proficiency lesson, which Mr Spokewheel had felt nervous about all week, she was most careful and sensible, and everything went well. She concentrated hard on putting the brakes on and getting off, and her cycling showed definite improvement.

The following Saturday, she turned out holding her board with its poster saying 'BRING BACK BIKES'. Behind her came Blossom with red stickers saying 'BIKES, BIKES, BIKES' all over hers. Thomas had refused to join in; he said that they ought to wait for Tamworth to return and he went to see Henry instead.

Down the street trotted Great Aunt Hattie on her short legs. She was wearing a new, pink hat held on with green hatpins, and was singing 'Bring Back Bikes' to the tune of 'Land of Hope and Glory'. Behind her wobbled Blossom on her bike, trying to go slowly and feeling a complete fool. This was very different from marching along with Tamworth and all his friends. Here she felt conspicuous and silly, and Thomas wasn't there with her. She wished she hadn't agreed to Great Aunt Hattie's plan. For when

Tamworth marched along, such was his personality that people often joined, whether they had intended to or not. But no one joined Great Aunt Hattie and Blossom.

People doing their afternoon shopping just stared at them as if they were mad. Then Blossom caught sight of Deadly, Lurcher Dench's brother, with his gang. They were laughing and Blossom shivered for she was scared of Deadly.

He shouted to them, 'That's not a bad idea.'

He meant to be friendly, Blossom thought, and smiled nervously back. Just then Christopher Robin Baggs, Gwendolyn Twitchie and Crasher Dench came round the corner. They all giggled when they saw Great Aunt Hattie. Blossom wished that Lurcher was with them as he was always on her side.

'Great Aunt Hattie's batty,' sang out Christopher Robin.

'Batty and scatty,' added Gwendolyn.

'Potty and grotty,' called Crasher.

'Batty Hattie,' they chorused together.

Great Aunt Hattie didn't even notice. On she marched, waving her banner, while Blossom's face flamed red. The jeers and cries grew louder. Then the slow pace finally proved too much for Blossom; her front wheel spun on a can left carelessly in the road, and off she toppled. The bike fell on the ground, wheels spinning. Christopher Robin's gang roared with laughter, then they jumped up and down with glee. Tears stained Blossom's cheeks. Slowly she stood up. One leg was bleeding and her knuckles were skinned. Great Aunt Hattie still marched on, oblivious of Blossom's plight. It seemed to her that the whole world was making fun of her.

'I'm never ever working for a cause again,' Blossom promised herself.

But, suddenly, like a fiery comet, arms waving, cheeks red with rage, Thomas appeared, ever ready for a fight. Henry was at his side.

'Down with Baggsy!' they yelled.

'Spiflicate them!' Henry shouted.

'Exterminate them!' roared Thomas.

The group, never noted for its courage, scattered and fled, except for Crasher, who stood his ground, for all the Denches were noted fighters. But even he ran when, with yet another bloodcurdling yell, his brother Lurcher, pedalling at furious speed on his antique velocipede, headed for Crasher, crying, 'Leave Blossom alone!'

Dropping his machine to the ground Lurcher stepped forward ready for a scrap, but there was no one to attack for they'd all scarpered. Both disappointed, Thomas and Lurcher turned on one another and delivered a few blows, until Lurcher cried out, 'I'm on your side, stupid.'

'So you are,' Thomas agreed. 'Come on, let's buy some crisps instead.'

Blossom watched them go. They'd been ready to come to her aid, but now she was completely forgotten. She sighed, and picked up her bicycle which was still in one piece. Great Aunt Hattie was now a long way ahead, but the sound of her singing wafted faintly back.

Wheeling her bike, miserably and painfully, Blossom went home.

Later in the day, Great Aunt Hattie came home with PC Cubbins. 'I don't think she should be in the street causing a disturbance, so I brought her back to you,' he announced.

'I wasn't causing a disturbance. I'm causing a cause,' the old lady said defiantly. She came just about up to PC Cubbins's knees.

He spoke patiently to her. 'Well, ma'am, I think you'd be better employed taking up a suitable hobby, like knitting or gardening.'

'Fiddlesticks! Never. I've always detested knitting and I cannot *stand* flowers. I like excitement.'

'Well, I'm just giving you a gentle warning. No more disturbances.' He said goodbye and left.

'I'm not taking any notice of what he says,' said Great Aunt Hattie, flouncing upstairs.

But Thomas followed her. 'Excuse me, Great Aunt Hattie,' he said, 'but I do think you're just a bit old for this sort of thing. You'd better leave it to Tamworth. He's the expert.'

She thought about this for a moment and then shook her head. 'Rubbish,' she said.

*

One day next week a letter arrived from Cousin
Winifred, saying that she did not wish to cause
trouble, but she had discovered that her favourite
cactus plant, a hot-water bottle, a portrait of Winston
Churchill, and a sword in a scabbard were all missing
from her house. She imagined that Great Aunt Hattie
had removed them when she left. She, Cousin
Winifred, would call over in a day or two, bring them
some produce from her garden, and take back the
missing articles. And she hoped the old lady was
keeping well and not causing too much work.

Daddy and Mummy looked at one another. When
the old lady came down to breakfast, Mummy asked
her gently about the missing things, whereupon
Great Aunt Hattie burst into loud sobs. First she said
that it wasn't anything to do with her, then she
confessed that it was, declaring that it was all because
she hadn't enough money to give as many presents
as she wanted.

When Blossom came down to find her great-aunt in
tears she cried as well. Hearing that Great Aunt
Hattie didn't have much money, Blossom fetched
down her savings box – a toffee tin – and offered her
the twenty-three pence it contained. Great Aunt
Hattie cried even louder, and said that she would
have to go. Mummy consoled her and they all had a
cup of tea, while Daddy went thankfully to work.

Thomas kept well out of the way, having no

intention of offering his money to anyone. He knew what he wanted to buy with it – a new cricket bat.

'What a fuss they're making downstairs,' he said to Hedgecock and Mr Rab.

'I wish you'd deal with that cat today,' Hedgecock grumbled. 'Like you said you would. He was horrible to us yesterday.'

'He made some really unforgivable remarks,' quavered Mr Rab. 'I can hardly bear to repeat them.'

'I can. He said you were a long, stupid piece of shivery jelly,' Hedgecock said.

'Oh, oh! How can you bear to say it?'

'Very easily. He called me a grizzly bit of stupid make-believe,' snapped Hedgecock. 'What I'd like to do to him! But he's so quick. Too fast for me.'

'I promise you I'll settle him,' Thomas replied. 'But he must be hiding from me, for I never see him nowadays.'

'How I wish he'd never come here,' Mr Rab sighed.

'Thomas, you'll be very late if you don't get up. Come on,' called his mother, putting an end to the conversation.

Chapter Nine

Tamworth returned to Pig House fresh from his triumph at saving the beautiful tree-filled valley from being filled up with rubble to make into a car park. He told Blossom and Thomas and Melanie all about it as they gathered round him.

'Oh, you are so wonderful,' Melanie murmured lovingly. 'There's no one like you, Tamworth. No other pig like you in the whole wide world.'

Then they told him about the failure of Great Aunt Hattie's efforts at campaigning so far.

'You'll have to come and lend a trotter,' Thomas said. 'She hasn't a clue about how to go on.'

'Certainly,' Tamworth cried. 'I've already ordered a bicycle, specially built for me. It should be here next week, and you can teach me how to ride it.'

'You on a bike. That should be good for a laugh.' Thomas grinned.

'Don't be impertinent, dear boy,' the giant pig replied. 'I shall look very handsome on a bicycle.'

*

Back at home the children found someone with Mummy and Great Aunt Hattie. The woman had a large white face, rather like a balloon, and wore a mustard-coloured, hand-knitted suit that showed her bulges, and purple stockings. Cousin Winifred had come to visit Great Aunt Hattie and to collect the objects removed by her for presents.

'Oh yes, I've definitely got green fingers,' she was saying as the children went in. Thomas looked at them. They looked perfectly ordinary to him. Just the usual colour. Grown-ups were peculiar. Fancy sitting there saying you'd got green fingers. It was stupid to say that, even if you were unlucky enough to have them, but if you hadn't, it was just plain ridiculous.

Blossom sat staring at her great-aunt. At last, during a pause in the conversation, she asked, 'Why are you wearing two hats, Great Aunt Hattie?'

'Nonsense. I'm only wearing one hat. Now why on earth should I be wearing two hats?'

'That's what I wondered,' Blossom replied.

Her mother whispered, 'I've told her, but she takes no notice.'

'She's like that,' Cousin Winifred remarked, drawing in her lips.

Great Aunt Hattie is wearing two hats because she doesn't like Cousin Winifred, Blossom thought. And I don't like her either.

Thomas didn't care for Cousin Winifred at all, but

since there was hardly anyone he liked, he was used
to the feeling.

'Touch your head, and then you'll know you've got
two hats on,' he suggested, trying to be helpful
among these people with green fingers and two hats.

'I have no intention of touching my head to see if
there are two hats there,' snapped his great-aunt. 'I
don't do that kind of thing when there's company.'

Cousin Winifred breathed heavily so that all her
bulges rippled. Thomas watched fascinated. Really,
she was just like a whale. She whispered out of the

70

side of her mouth to Mummy, who looked red and uncomfortable.

'She's absolutely batty, you know. Should be put away.'

'Oh no,' Mummy murmured unhappily.

Cousin Winifred turned and said very loudly, as if the old lady were deaf, 'Now, what's all this I hear about your cycling? Fine sight you must look at your age, in your two hats, I suppose. Well, take care you don't fall off. Bones don't mend easily at your time in life.'

A great gloom seemed to have descended on them all. Then in walked Daddy, smiling and looking very cheerful.

'Hello, Cousin Winifred,' he boomed. 'Are those your cabbages in the kitchen? Thank you. Magnificent. Magnificent. You've definitely got green fingers. Aunt, you look so pretty in one hat, I don't know why you're wearing two, though you look very nice in them.'

And he smiled at her in a way that made Blossom think that he must have been handsome in his youth, a long time ago in the dark ages.

Great Aunt Hattie smiled up at him. 'Was I wearing two? How silly of me. I'll take one off at once.'

And she did so, taking out the three hatpins and sticking them in the arm of the chair from where once again Mummy hastily removed them. Thomas got up to go out. Mad, all of them, quite mad, he decided.

He went to the shed and got out his cricket bat, neglected through the football season. It was too small, for he was a lot bigger than he had been last year when he hadn't played much, anyway, as he'd been too young to be any good. But this year he'd show them. He was sure that he could hit the ball harder and further than Lurcher Dench could. When he'd got his new bat he'd hit century after century, fours and sixes galore. He hit an imaginary six, knocking three buds off his mother's favourite rose bush.

Bowling too; he must work hard at that this year. It must be absolutely great to be a fast bowler, shattering wicket after wicket, the batsman standing in his crease trembling. What had happened to last year's ball, he wondered?

Back into the shed he went, to search for it. He looked in all the corners but there was no sign of a cricket ball. As he came out of the shed he noticed that it looked a bit of a mess, so he picked up the pot of paint he'd knocked over and tried to wipe it up with an oily rag, but the splodge on the floor only grew larger and oilier. Several of Dad's tools seemed to be lying in the paint.

Sighing, Thomas made his way to Blossom's room, where he quickly found her tennis ball, and then returned to the garden to practise his fast bowling.

Mummy had said that he couldn't play football in the garden, but she hadn't said anything about cricket. Not lately anyway. Now, if he could practise both batting and bowling, he could become Thomas the great all-rounder. He'd run up to the wicket – and what was that movement for over-arm bowling? Surely he could remember it. Let's see. Lift left arm high in front, bring right arm back and round and over, like a windmill, and let the ball go.

The ball went. There followed a resounding crash and a series of tinkles which didn't sound at all like music to Thomas's ears. The kitchen window was shattered and glass lay in shining shapes everywhere. Nor was that all. The flying ball appeared to have crashed into something in the kitchen as well.

He waited for someone to come.

They *must* have heard. No one could have missed

that awful din. But no one appeared. No angry figure. No raised voice. Thomas knew he ought to tell his mother. He'd always been encouraged to own up. But he couldn't face standing in front of Cousin Winifred and confessing that he'd just broken the window. No, he would go back to Tamworth, and forget his problems. By the time he came back to face the music at least Cousin Winifred would have gone.

Chapter Ten

Now he was back at home, Tamworth lost no time in organizing this new campaign. First of all he called in Mr Rab to write something for posters and leaflets. These were redesigned by Blossom, and this time, inspired by the great pig, she excelled herself with a wonderful drawing of Tamworth cycling through the countryside on a May afternoon in England. It was covered with trees and flowers and animals and birds, and she painted Tamworth in a glowing red-gold colour that took her ages to get exactly right. Along the road on which Tamworth cycled, Mr Rab's words appeared.

> Given a bicycle you can ride
> All over the countryside,
> Bikes are jolly, bikes are fun,
> They'll give joy to everyone.

'Its a bit plain,' Mr Rab had said. 'I'm not quite sure about it.'

'It will do beautifully,' Tamworth said firmly.

'But I do like something really grand. Like an epic

poem.' Mr Rab sighed deeply. 'I never finished mine. That beastly cat ruined my concentration. He made me too unhappy to write.'

'Never mind, when we've finished the campaign, you can go back to it.'

'But we never seem to finish campaigns,' said Mr Rab. 'Or at least, when we've finished one, then we start fighting another. There's never any of the peace and quiet necessary for a poet.'

'Peace and quiet, fiddlesticks!' snorted Hedgecock, who could bear Mr Rab's conversation no longer. 'The only useful thing that you ever do in the whole of your pink-nosed life is to write the odd word for Tamworth. Not that any of it is up to much as far as I can see, for I've always thought that poetry is just a lot of rubbish, but if it's all right for Tamworth, then it will do. Now let's get down to the really important things. How many leaflets do we need?'

Tamworth mentioned a large number that made Hedgecock whistle with delight, and he immediately went into facts and figures and calculations and costs so that his crotchety face looked almost happy for once.

Blossom drew a smaller picture of Tamworth, this time to print on leaflets in black and white only, as coloured ones cost a lot. Thomas had drawn some pictures of a penny-farthing bike with Mr Rab and Hedgecock on it. This made them very pleased. On

them he wrote: 'Don't walk, don't drive. Ride a bike!'

Tamworth called his friend Owly, who promised to get the birds to deliver the leaflets all over the country, right up to the wild mountains where the eagles and buzzards would carry on with the task.

Then he asked the Vicar's wife to tea, and they arranged that she should make another recording. Quite soon afterwards she was heard singing on the radio:

> 'Daisy, Daisy, give me your answer do,
> I'm half crazy all for the love of you.

It won't be a stylish marriage,
I can't afford a carriage.
But you'll look sweet upon the seat
Of a bicycle made for two.'

This recording proved to be more popular even than her 'Save the Trees' song, and soon she began to earn a lot of money.

'If this goes on you'll become a millionaire,' the Vicar said to her sternly.

He didn't think that they ought to be rich. The Vicar's wife hung her head, and he spoke more kindly.

'Never mind, we'll give it all away to charity, and then it will be all right.'

'Do you think I could just have a new dress?' she asked bravely.

'What, another one? You know my ideas on personal vanity.'

'I haven't had one since the red velvet one I bought with my "Save the Trees" record,' the Vicar's wife said even more bravely, for the Vicar was a very tall man.

'Well yes, then. But not so bright this time. Something suitable, brown or grey or dark blue.'

So the Vicar's wife went with Mummy to buy a dress, grew most excited and finally bought a long one as gloriously golden as Tamworth, and covered with embroidery from top to toe.

'It's not the kind of dress that I should have bought,' she said, holding her parcel lovingly as they came out of the shop. 'But it's very beautiful.'

Tamworth appeared on *Blue Peter* speaking enthusiastically about cycling and looking handsome as usual.

Generally things were well in hand and all the preparations for the march were under way. By now, Tamworth's marches were widely known and it was likely that people would turn up to see this one as they would a carnival. But there was just one snag. Tamworth had imagined himself leading the procession, a fine golden pig on his bicycle, looking the image of the pig in Blossom's picture. Unfortunately he seemed quite unable to master the art of cycling.

Whether it was his weight or his trotters that caused the difficulty, it was difficult to tell. But the fact remained that, a week before the march was to be held, Tamworth had no more idea of how to ride a bike than he had of standing on his snout.

Again and again they tried to get him going. Thomas, Blossom, Great Aunt Hattie, Lurcher Dench, Henry, Farmer Baggs (when he had the time) all stood round him, holding up the machine, trying to support Tamworth's great weight, placing his trotters on the pedals and handlebars, and shouting words of encouragement.

'Come on, now. It's really very easy. Remember the cause. Just push now and off you go.'

And off he usually went in a heavy heap on the ground. Despite failures, he persevered, until one evening, descending weightily to the ground yet once more, he nearly squashed Melanie. After she had been comforted by Blossom, Joe, the shire horse, who had also been helping, spoke out in his slow, heavy way:

"Twoant do, Tamworth. 'Twoant do.'

'What 'twoant do?' asked that pig irritably. He'd got a lot of bruises.

'What 'twoant do is the riding of that there machine by 'ee, Tamworth,' Joe said patiently. 'You'm the wrong shape for it. Stands to reason. Pigs weren't meant to fly and pigs weren't meant to go gallivantin' around the countryside on bicycles.'

It was a long speech for Joe and Tamworth's feelings were deeply hurt at the end of it. He turned pale and sat staring sadly into space for some time. Blossom ran to him and wrapped her arms around his neck, for she could not bear anyone to be unhappy, especially Tamworth. At last he spoke.

'I've always been able to do what humans do. I'm as clever as they are . . .'

'Cleverer,' Thomas said, stroking the furry ears.

'. . . I can write and play football and talk and sing . . .'

'Mm. Your singing's pretty awful,' Thomas commented.

Tamworth went even paler. It seemed to be a time for truth telling and he wasn't enjoying it much.

'I shall have to give up the idea of riding at the head of the procession on my bike,' he said at last. 'It does seem a pity. I was looking forward to it.'

Everyone started talking at once, full of ideas, mostly suggestions as to who should be leader, usually themselves.

'Quiet,' Tamworth ordered. 'Let me think.'

Great Aunt Hattie jumped up and down on her little legs. 'I think I know what would work,' she cried.

'What?'

'Wait and see. I'm not sure about it yet.'

And away she stamped humming 'Onward Christian Soldiers' very loudly.

Chapter Eleven

'What a magnificent thing,' Tamworth cried.
'Wherever did you get it from? It's a masterpiece.'

'It's on loan from the Museum, and it's the only
one of its kind in the country. It was built by an
enthusiast about fifty years ago. And I've got it for
you for a whole month,' said Great Aunt Hattie.

'It's a funny bike,' Thomas said. 'It's got three
wheels.'

'It's a giant-size tricycle,' cried Tamworth. 'And
what a fine machine it is. Just look at it. Clever
Hattie!'

They beamed at each other.

'What a bell,' Thomas cried, ringing it.

They all crowded round admiring the gleaming
spokes, the patterned leather saddle, the polished
lamps, the size of it.

'Are you going to try it?'

'Well, I haven't really time now. There is a meeting
of the Conservation Society Tree Department this
evening and I must shortly be on my way.
Accompany me a short distance along the lane,

Thomas, if you will. Melanie, my dear, I shan't be late home. Perhaps you would look after that wonderful tricycle, dear lady,' he said to Great Aunt Hattie. 'And thank you very much for it.'

Thomas mounted on Tamworth's back and away they went.

As Thomas and Tamworth went down the lane, Tamworth said, 'I didn't want to try it out in front of everybody like that, as I was afraid I might fall off again. If you will come with me, just the two of us, tomorrow, we'll find a quiet spot where I can master this difficult art with no one watching.'

Thomas nodded.

After Tamworth had gone to the meeting, Thomas walked slowly home, idly slashing nettles with a

stick. It was too hot to run. The sky hung heavy and grey. Thunder was in the air. In the kitchen he drank three glasses of water, then went slowly up the stairs, sitting on each step in turn. He would lie on the bed and read for a bit, he thought, as he went to push open his bedroom door. Then he paused and listened. Someone, inside the room, was talking in a slow, sinister voice.

'I'm so sorry for you two poor thing, prrhhh,' the voice purred. 'What a miserrrrable life you lead, prrhhh, stuffed sillies that you are. You have to wait for Thomas to take you out with him, prrhhh, while I, I am free as the wind, to go where I please, prrhhhh, to chase birds and climb trees, to walk over the rooftops with my tail waving, and to kill mice, mrrhhh. Oh, the sublime joy of chasing a tiny, furry

mouse with its long, long tail, prrrhhhh, then lying still as a stone, until, prrhhh, it thinks you've forgotten it, mrrh, as if you ever could, and so he runs this way and that trying, hoping to escape, prrrhhhp, but there I am, with my steel claws in my velvet paws, mrh, mrh, and then sccccttt, I leap on it, and it knows there is no escape ever, prrrhhh, prrrhhhh.'

Thomas was about to burst in on this frightful speech, when he heard Hedgecock speak up.

'I'm glad to say that me and Mr Rab 'ud rather not know how to torture and kill like that, thank you, cat. And now, go away will you? We don't like you and we don't want to have anything to do with you.'

'I don't know how that nice lady came to have a beastly pet like you,' Mr Rab burst out.

'She thinks I'm a lovely pussy cat,' purred the animal. 'No one knows what I'm really like except you two, and I'm going to make you so afraid of me, pprrhhh, that you won't tell, you silly, stuffed things.'

'I'm not stuffed,' Mr Rab cried piteously. 'I'm not stuffed, I tell you.'

Thomas could bear no more. He flung open the door and charged at Vespa, who streaked over to the window and leapt out.

'I hope you break your neck,' Thomas shouted, but the cat had landed safely on the ground and, with a contemptuous hiss, vanished into the undergrowth.

Thomas stormed downstairs, face red, eyes ablaze, Thomas in one of his furies.

'You've got to get rid of that horrible animal of yours. He's a monster,' he shouted at Great Aunt Hattie.

'How dare you speak like that to your great-aunt? Just apologize at once,' Daddy snapped.

Quite patiently for him, Thomas said, 'I didn't mean to be rude, but that wicked cat is tormenting Hedgecock and Mr Rab and making them unhappy.'

'But I'm sure that my dear pussy cat wouldn't do anything like that,' said the old lady. Mummy joined in: 'He always seems to be quite a nice cat to me.'

'Nice cat . . .?' Thomas said incredulously.

'Yes, he's very clean.'

Thomas opened his mouth to speak, and then closed it again. It was a waste of time talking to grown-ups. They never understood about real problems. All they thought about was cleanliness and tidiness and rubbish like that. Clean cat, indeed. Here, in this very house, was the wickedest cat in the world, but grown-ups thought it was a good cat because it was clean. To Thomas this fact was a further proof of Vespa's villainy. He ran out into the garden, grey and still and steamy under the gloomy sky.

He picked up a pebble and threw it at the apple

87

tree. Something stirred on one of the branches, a darker shadow in the gathering gloom. Yellow eyes glinted. Thomas threw another pebble. Vespa reared up and arched, spitting viciously.

'Bull's-eye,' Thomas yelled victoriously.

'Whatever are you doing?' Blossom cried, appearing at that moment. 'Throwing stones like that?'

'That animal up there is the wickedest creature that

ever lived. Go away you horrible beast. Go away and never come back.'

Thomas aimed another pebble at the tree, and Vespa, with back and belly low on the ground, shot to safety.

As he leapt on to the wall, he hissed, 'I'll get you lot for this.'

Chapter Twelve

That night when Thomas went to bed Hedgecock and
Mr Rab were missing; no little figures squabbling, no
one counting blanket squares, no one singing Mr
Rab's Bedtime song. Where were they? What were
they playing at? I'll get them for this, Thomas
thought. They ought to be here, getting ready to
settle for the night.

He looked in the bedclothes, then under the bed.
No sign of the stripy fellow or the feathery-prickled
one. He flung open his wardrobe door and a pile of
T-shirts, trainers, boxes, old boots and jeans fell out
all over him, but no Hedgecock, no Mr Rab. He
jammed everything back in the wardrobe and leaned
against the doors to shut them. They didn't close, but
Thomas didn't care. He was getting worried. Where
could they be? He flung all the toys out of the old
toybox he'd painted long ago. Not there. He left them
on the floor where they were soon joined by all the
clothes in the chest of drawers, well, all those that
weren't hanging over the edges and cascading out of
corners. He looked behind his chair, then pulled back

the curtains to see if they were sitting on the sill looking out of the window – though why they should be doing that he didn't know, except that they were both barmy.

At the end of ten minutes Thomas was sure they weren't in the bedroom and the room looked like nothing you've ever seen. He was very angry.

He stormed into Blossom's room shouting, 'Come on, what have you done with them?' and was surprised to see Great Aunt Hattie sitting up in bed reading. He'd forgotten that she'd be there.

'What have I done with what, Edward?' asked his great-aunt, looking over not one but two pairs of spectacles, one at the top and one at the tip of her nose.

'Where's Blossom? Where's Hedgecock? Where's Mr Rab?' Thomas rattled off like a machine gun. 'And my name's Thomas, not Edward.'

He was by now afraid, and the more frightened he grew, the angrier he became.

'Blossom's downstairs reading, I think. I don't know where your toys are.'

'She's no right to be downstairs reading and they're not my toys, they're Hedgecock and Mr Rab and THEY OUGHT TO BE ON MY BED!'

He was shouting his head off and his mother appeared.

'What's all that noise? What are you shouting for?

And being rude to your great-aunt.'

'He's being rude because he's angry. Dear Edward was always angry.'

'I don't care tuppence for Edward, what's he got to do with it? Mum, somebody's stolen Hedgecock and Mr Rab and you've got to get them back for me.'

'Nobody's likely to steal them, for heaven's sake,' said his father, also appearing. 'They're not exactly valuable, are they?'

'They are to Thomas,' said Mummy. 'Come on, we'll help you to find them. I bet you left them in the garden.'

Then she spotted his bedroom.

'Oh, dear,' she sighed. 'Right, come on everybody. Blossom! Come here! Let's get going. Aunt Hattie, you've got two pairs of spectacles on your nose.'

'I shall need them for searching,' said the old girl, skipping neatly from her bed.

Thomas could remember Mr Rab and Hedgecock being with him in the garden while he checked his bike tyres. Then he had leapt on the bike and ridden away, forgetting about Hedgecock and Mr Rab until he went to bed. Now they weren't in the house or in the garden. Everywhere had been searched, and it was growing dark.

'Let's pack it in and have another go in the morning,' said Daddy.

'But I can't sleep without them and they can't sleep without me,' wailed Thomas, full of guilt and misery. 'They must be ever so scared, wherever they are.'

His father breathed heavily and closed his eyes.

'I shall go demented,' he said through his teeth.

'I know! They must be at Pig House. I must have left them there. Come on, Dad, Mum. Let's go.'

'Look, it's getting late and Tamworth may not want to be disturbed.'

'No, he won't mind. Come on, come on. Quickly. Please. Please. Please, please, please.'

'Let's go,' Blossom said. 'We might as well or he'll go on and on.'

But Hedgecock and Mr Rab weren't at Pig House. They seemed to have disappeared for ever from the face of the earth.

'We've got to get the police,' said Thomas. He was nearly in tears, Thomas who never cried.

'Tomorrow, Thomas, tomorrow,' whispered his mother.

It was really dark by now and difficult to search even with a torch. Thomas at last let himself be led back to bed, worn out. As he fell asleep his last thought was, 'In the morning, in the morning. I'll find them in the morning . . .'

*

In the middle of the night Thomas woke up. Outside, the moon had risen filling the garden with silver light. He pulled on his jeans and sweater and trainers and slipped out of the house as silent as a ghost. Through the garden he went and as he paused by the gate he caught sight of the shadow of a tail . . . a cat's tail, high in the air.

Staying in the shadows he slipped along, following the tail that looked like a flag, upright and important.

After a few minutes he realized where they were heading – Baggs's farm. The cat ran faster on little,

pleased paws. Almost, Thomas thought, he could hear purring. The moon shone so brightly he could see clearly with no danger of falling and the cat didn't look round.

The cat and the boy made their way round to the back of the farm where the cat sprang neatly up some steps and into a barn whose door was ajar.

As quietly as he could Thomas followed, slipping through the door to hear:

'You stupid, stuffed creatures. Don't you look silly stuck in there? You can't escape, can you? No one will ever find you here and that terrible boy will be miserable! Serves him right for throwing pebbles at me!'

'That's where you're wrong,' cried Thomas, flinging himself at the cat, who flattened himself, stabbed him with his claws, then shot out of the door as if chased by demons.

But Thomas didn't follow. He was much too busy getting Hedgecock and Mr Rab out of the cat basket in which they'd been imprisoned, their heads sticking pitifully out of the hole at the top, too small for them to get out of.

'I kept myself brave by reciting all the poetry I knew,' quavered Mr Rab as they were carried home by Thomas, running as fast as he could.

'Yes, that was worse than being shut in. But I recited all the swear words I know,' growled Hedgecock.

Safe in bed they told Thomas what had happened. Vespa had been tormenting them as usual in the garden and who should pass by but Christopher Robin Baggs, who looked round to see if anyone was watching and then made off with them, hiding them to torment Thomas. The cat had followed, of course, to torment them further.

'Sing the Bedtime song, Mr Rab,' said Thomas, not caring if he was too old for it these days.

'Bedtime rubbish,' growled Hedgecock, and started to count his squares diagonally till they all fell asleep.

Chapter Thirteen

What was ever after known as the Big Bike Ride made
its way along the road towards the fair some days
later. Tamworth had decided that the old lady should
lead it after all, and there she was, bloomers a-ripple
in the breeze, flower-covered hat tied on with scarlet
ribbons, little legs a-pedalling. It was a farewell
occasion for Great Aunt Hattie because she'd
received an invitation to stay with an old friend in
Devon, and was to leave quite soon. She was sorry to
go, but Thomas and Blossom would visit her in the
summer. She had never really understood about the
disappearance of Vespa, and still called, 'Puss, puss,
puss,' every evening. But Lurcher Dench had
promised her one of their latest batch of kittens,
which would soon be old enough to leave its mother.
So this was very much Great Aunt Hattie's day and
she sang 'She Who Would Valiant Be' at the top of
her voice as she rode along.

Behind her came Thomas and most of the school
cyclists on an extraordinary collection of veteran and
vintage bikes on loan from the Museum. Astride a

penny-farthing rode Lurcher Dench, this one being
the most difficult to ride and Lurcher generally
reckoned to be the most skilful cyclist among them, to
Thomas's private annoyance. Mr Spokewheel rode a
boneshaker, with enormous pride and some
discomfort. This was the oldest bicycle, dating from
the eighteen sixties, and extremely valuable, as were
many of the others. PC Spriggs and PC Cubbins
drove along in their Escort just behind the Museum
entries, to ensure that none of them went missing,
lost, stolen or strayed.

The Vicar's wife was mounted on a sit up and beg
bike, with a curved crossbar, just like the one she'd
had when she was young. There were tall bikes,
small bikes, mountain bikes and racing bikes with
dropped handlebars that could travel at breathtaking
speeds; Thomas was riding one of these, to his
delight, though he had to moderate his speed to that
of the fleet. Choppers, scooters, two tandems, one
ridden by Mrs Postlewaithe and Mummy, the other
by Crasher and Nosher Dench, black bikes, red bikes,
green bikes, silver bikes, a whole galaxy of them.

Behind these came Joe, the shire horse, drawing a
beautiful old wagon lent by Farmer Baggs, painted in
crimson and yellow, and decorated with green
ribbons like the ones Blossom had lovingly and
somewhat unevenly plaited into Joe's mane and tail.
And in the wagon sat Melanie and Tamworth's

piglets, now living in their own homes but who'd all returned for this special occasion. Albert the youngest, the runt, was now the biggest and bossiest. He was black all over and waved like the Queen Mother as they went along.

Fanny Cow and Barry MacKenzie Goat followed, with Ethel Everready and Owly perched on their backs. Owly was asleep, actually, as it was a very bright day.

But the highlight appeared right at the end. On hearing of the Big Bike Ride, the curator of a London museum had sent the most marvellous machine of all, a huge tricycle, built for eight, and there rode Tamworth with Mr Starling, Thomas's teacher, Henry and his father, the professor, who had just decided to write a history of bicycles, Hedgecock and Mr Rab, Gwendolyn Twitchie, all smiles and yellow curls. And then, of course, there was Blossom, holding her marvellous banner of Tamworth riding an ordinary bike, which, as Tamworth said, alas, would never come true. Still he looked full of good humour as he pedalled along with all the other cyclists.

Mr Rab thought of Vespa as they went along. He didn't know why, it was a pity to spoil so pleasant a day, but he couldn't help remembering Hedgecock's and his ordeal. After their rescue, Tamworth had called an extraordinary meeting of the Animals'

Union, with instructions to capture one cat and bring him back for trial. Birds delivered messages throughout the country, but of Vespa there was no sign. Posters appeared on poles with a description, but days passed and no one reported any news of him, though it was rumoured that a cat named Vespa was alive and well and living in Cornwall. On investigation, however, Vespa turned out to be a female cat, and just about to produce kittens. By the time the day for the Big Bike Ride came most people had forgotten about Vespa, but not Mr Rab. Then Blossom turned to smile at him so he started to make up a poem instead.

Blossom was thinking, Great Aunt Hattie is leaving soon and I shall miss her. But I won't think about that now. I'll think about the sunshine and the march, all the people waving, and smiling and the party we'll have tonight with all the piglets.

The strains of the Vicar's wife singing 'Daisy, Daisy' floated back on the breeze and they all rode onward to the fair.

And what was Thomas thinking? Who knows?